Today is Tom's birthday. He would
love to have fish for supper.

Molly has another idea. She would like to bake Tom a cake!

Just in case, they put on aprons.

Then it's off to the refrigerator . . .

Now, to work!

Tom is very good at mixing.

Help! The little bird has fallen in.

No bother! Molly and Tom rescue him.

Tom adds a little pepper.
Oh, well. It **is** Tom's cake!

Finally the cake is ready. All the dolls
are invited to the party.

But Tom thinks the cake is not quite finished.

They aren't **real** fish,
but they will taste delicious!